Lizzie McGuire

A VERY LiZZiE CHRISTMAS

Adapted by Jasmine Jones
Based on the series created by Terri Minsky
Part One is based on a teleplay written
by Douglas Tuber & Tim Maile.
Part Two is based on a teleplay written
by Nina G. Bargiel & Jeremy J. Bargiel.

Watch it on

Disney CHANNEL

abc Kids

Disney PRESS

VOLO

New York

Printed in the United States of America

First Edition
1 3 5 7 9 10 8 6 4 2

Library of Congress Catalog Card Number: 2002105337

ISBN 0-7868-4617-8
For more Disney Press fun, visit www.disneybooks.com
Visit DisneyChannel.com

PART ONE

CHAPTER ONE

"Ho, ho, ho!" Santa said as he accepted a wrapped gift from Larry Tudgeman. "Merry Christmas, son. Merry Christmas."

Hillridge Junior High's "Holiday Cheer-ity Drive" was off to a great start. "Santa" had spent the last hour collecting toys for needy children. And, at this point, he had enough to fill, like, *several* sleighs.

Lizzie McGuire thought this year's Santa the oddest-looking Claus she'd ever seen.

True, he had the traditional red suit and fake beard. But this guy was younger than most Santas—on the skinny side, too. And his long brown hair stuck out from beneath his red cap. Actually, this guy looked more like a rock star wearing a really strange disguise than like a guy playing Santa.

"Ho, ho, ho," Larry said cheerfully. "And a bottle of rum!" He laughed at his own joke, and then he stopped. "Oh, wait," Larry said, "that's pirates." He shrugged. "Though pirates have beards and so does Santa, so I'm stickin' with it."

As Larry walked off, Lizzie sighed from her place on the line in front of Santa. Did Larry really have to be so nerd-tacular? Even during the Christmas season? Couldn't he take a vacation, like everyone else?

Lizzie looked over at her friend David "Gordo" Gordon, who was waiting with her.

He didn't seem impatient. Lizzie sighed again and decided to try not to be such a grouch. But it wasn't easy. She and Gordo had been waiting forever. At least Larry's weirdness had been a distraction. Santa certainly seemed to agree—

"Weird kid," Santa said as he gazed after Larry.

Santa's "elf" assistant nodded. He was older than Santa. A lot older. Like Social Security old. And he was wearing a dark green vest. "You got that right, Santa," said the senior citizen elf.

"Although—" Santa mused, "who am I to talk?" He smiled and went back to his Kris Kringle shtick. "Ho, ho, ho. Merry Christmas, Merry Christmas."

Gordo turned to Lizzie. "So, how are we rating this year's Santa?" he asked.

"Well," Lizzie said as she eyed the Santa

again, "off the beaten path, scraggly beard, and no gut."

"Good attitude, though," Gordo said as the Santa sat there, ho-ho-hoing his head off. "I think the Santa from last year was in a motorcycle gang."

Lizzie nodded. Last year's Santa had been a huge, scary-looking guy wearing a red cap and a denim vest over his ripped jeans. He had grabbed the donated packages as though he were planning to sell the toys on eBay five minutes after everyone left.

Lizzie sighed and adjusted her grip on the dark blue laundry sack she was carrying. It was so heavy it nearly slipped out of her hands.

Gordo eyed the bag. "What is all that junk?" he asked.

"A drum, a compressed-air horn, a hand buzzer, a siren hat, and a toy bugle," Lizzie replied. She pulled the siren hat out of the bag and showed it to Gordo.

Gordo's eyebrows drew together. "Aren't all of those Matt's things?" he asked.

Not so much his "things," thought Lizzie, as his torture devices. Who else but her *annoying* little brother would have such an *annoying* pile of stuff? "I think he's outgrown them," Lizzie told Gordo innocently. "Besides, he didn't say anything when I took them."

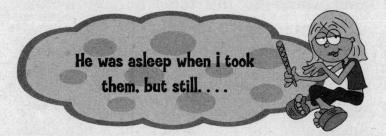

The line moved, and Lizzie and Gordo stepped forward. Lizzie struggled with the bag again. It was amazing how heavy some of these torture devices could be.

"You should've just donated your little brother," Gordo suggested. "He weighs a lot less."

"Yeah," Lizzie agreed. The truth was, she had thought about it—several times. But she figured that even a charity would reject him. Besides, she had another reason.

"But I need him to help me make some papier-mâché for my float on the Christmas parade. Plus, he's good at getting sticky stuff everywhere—so this time, he'll be useful." Lizzie grinned.

"I'm in charge of decorating the tree on the float, right?" Gordo asked. "'Cause, frankly, I've mastered making dreidels and lighting menorahs, and I'm looking for a new challenge."

Gordo was Jewish, but he didn't mind helping out with the Christmas spirit now and then. And Lizzie always went over to his house to light the candles on the last night of Hanukkah. Lizzie loved celebrating both holidays—it made the season seem even more special.

Lizzie smiled. "I think my float will keep you busy." Lizzie opened her bag and pulled out a drawing of her float. It showed several Christmas trees, snow, a life-sized cottage labeled "Santa's House," and giant candy canes everywhere. Large block letters at the top of the page screamed, ROCK 'N' ROLL XMAS!

"Rock 'n' Roll Christmas, huh?" Gordo said, looking at the paper. "You're really going for it."

"First prize is a ski trip," Lizzie said, grinning at the picture of her float. "I could get all Matt's noisy stuff out of the way *and* win a free trip to Aspen—this could be the best Christmas ever!" She smiled as she imagined herself in a cute ski outfit, zooming away from Matt at top speed. Now, *there* was a mental image to put her in the holiday spirit. I just love ski slopes, Lizzie thought.

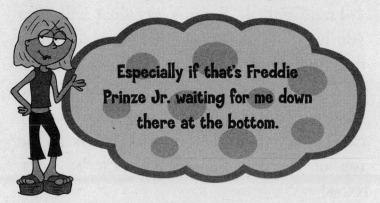

Especially if that's Freddie Prinze Jr. waiting for me down there at the bottom.

Lizzie was still smiling as she stepped up to the front of the line and hauled her sack over to Santa. His eyes went wide at the sight of the huge bag of toys.

"Ho, ho, ho!" Santa said. "Whoa, major loot." He pulled open the bag and pulled out a bright yellow construction hat with a red light on top. "Sweet siren hat."

"Oh, very generous," Santa's helper elf said. "Eh, Santa?"

"Believe me," Lizzie said to Santa and the elf, "it was my pleasure." She was particularly happy to see the siren hat go. There was no counting the number of Saturday mornings Matt had run into Lizzie's room with that hat on, screaming, "Rise and shine! Rise and shine!" *Ugh*.

Really, Matt should thank me, Lizzie thought. By giving these things away, I've probably just added several years to his life.

This is a good deed I would happily repeat, Lizzie thought. "The kids get a merry little Christmas, and I get a silent night," she added under her breath as she walked away.

And this is only Part One of Operation Best Christmas Ever, Lizzie thought. If things go according to plan, I should be rockin' around the Christmas tree . . . in Aspen!

❄ ❄ ❄

Lizzie had to admit—her float was looking good. Of course, that was only because she was looking at a watercolor painting she had made of what she wanted "Rock 'n' Roll Xmas" to look like. The real float was only a pile of junk on a trailer.

Lizzie was standing in a warehouse, surrounded by the sounds of drills and hammers going full tilt. It seemed like everyone Lizzie knew was working on a float for the Christmas parade. We're talking mucho competition, Lizzie thought as she looked around. But Lizzie had faith in her idea. And Gordo was there to help her.

Lizzie nodded at her painting. "So, we have to make this—"

"Out of this—" Gordo added, looking at the pile of chicken wire, candy canes, and plastic foam.

"Using this." Lizzie picked up a cardboard box overflowing with paste, newspaper, glitter, and green, red, and black felt.

Gordo shrugged. "Well," he said, pulling the newspaper from the top of the box, "I guess I'll tear up paper for some papier-mâché."

Lizzie pulled a piece of white paper covered in red ink out of the box. "Oh, use my history paper, please," Lizzie said, handing Gordo the paper. She rolled her eyes. "I do *not* want my parents to see that."

"Hey, guys," Larry said as he ran over. "Can you help me out? I need something for my float. You wouldn't happen to have an exhaust-assembly system for a Rebel Forces X-wing Fighter, would you?"

Lizzie gave Gordo a sideways look. Was Larry serious? "'Fraid not," Lizzie said, peering into her craft box. "We've got some green felt," she offered, pulling the fabric out of the box.

Larry took the felt. "I can make that work," he said.

"So, what's the theme of your float?" Gordo asked.

"Death Star Christmas," Larry said with a grin. Then he launched into his screechy Yoda impersonation. "A very shiny nose Rudolph had, yes. . . ." He laughed and gave Lizzie a little wave with the green felt, then scurried off to work on his bizarro float.

"Weird kid," Gordo said.

"Yeah," Lizzie agreed. What else could she say? Larry took being a dweeb to a whole new level.

Just then, Kate Sanders flounced into the warehouse with her cousin Amy. Kate was wearing an ivory lace top with a flowered skirt, and her nails looked freshly manicured.

Not exactly the ideal outfit for a day of pasting and hammering, Lizzie thought. But that wasn't a huge surprise. Kate was a Grade-A snob and thought of herself as queen of the school. She probably has a legion of fans to do all of the work for her, Lizzie decided, just as two burly guys walked up behind Kate. The men were wearing coveralls and tool belts, and Lizzie recognized them as Mr. McGuire's softball buddies, David and Jeremy.

"My float's over against that wall," Kate snapped at the two men. "Get to work."

Gordo gaped at her. "Kate, you're paying carpenters to build your float?"

Kate gave Gordo a disgusted look. "Get real." She waved impatiently. "My *dad's* paying them."

The burly carpenter named David nodded. "The float will depict an immense ladybug wearing a Santa cap, whilst stereo speakers broadcast cheery music of a Yuletide nature," he said with the seriousness of a *This Old House* host's announcing a major remodeling project.

"The title of the float," added David's partner, Jeremy, "is to be called 'Jingle Bug.'" Then he shrugged. "Kind of adorable."

Kate smiled proudly.

Amy cocked an eyebrow at Lizzie's sketches. "Uh, Rock 'n' Roll Christmas?" she scoffed. "Whatever. Our float cost six grand."

Lizzie's jaw dropped. Six thousand dollars? Why didn't Kate just *buy* a trip to Aspen?

Kate frowned at the carpenters. "You guys are on the clock," she said. "Get the lead out!" The two men scurried off to build the enormous, adorable ladybug. Kate and Amy pranced off after them. Lizzie could just picture them spending their day barking orders and exchanging makeup tips.

Lizzie bit her lip. "Okay, six grand," she said, gazing defeatedly at the paper in Gordo's hand. "But I think our float design is better than a Jingle Bug."

"And we know you'll beat Tudgeman," Gordo added, gesturing to where Larry stood, constructing a giant marsh scene complete with Yoda and R2D2 in a Santa cap. "He's got robots; you've got fake penguins. Who doesn't love penguins?"

"We elves aren't too wild about them," said a voice.

Lizzie and Gordo looked over to see the short, older guy who had been playing the elf at their school earlier that day. He was still wearing his green elf vest, although he had it on over a gray sweatshirt and black fanny pack. And he'd exchanged his green stocking cap with a red pom-pom for a red baseball hat. "Elves are allergic to penguins," the old man went on. "My pal, Little Blinky, turned red as a turkey gobbler."

Lizzie smiled. "Wait, weren't you Santa's helper at school?"

"Santa's chief elf, officially," the old man corrected. "Knobby Frosty Bump. Nice to meet you."

"What are you doing here?" Gordo asked.

"This is a Christmas parade," Knobby explained. "I'm Santa's helper. Well, where else would I be?"

"Well, maybe in the North Pole, making toys?" Lizzie suggested.

Knobby waved off the suggestion. "My crew has that covered," he said. "After we have our spring manager's meeting and set our production goals, I'm pretty much hands off." Suddenly, Lizzie heard an electronic tinkling that sounded a lot like "Jingle Bells."

"Oh, excuse me," Knobby said as he pulled

a red cell phone out of his fanny pack. "Sometimes my elves need to reach me." Knobby punched the TALK button as he sat down on the edge of Lizzie's float. "Hello?" he said into the phone. "He did what? Well, why'd he try to pet it?" Knobby sounded upset. "And tell Thimblemuffin to stop petting wild animals—if he loves animals so much, he can deworm Rudolph."

Lizzie grimaced. Now, there was a Christmas chore she wouldn't want.

"Oh, my goodness." Knobby shook his head and pressed the OFF button on his phone. "A badger bit Thimblemuffin," he explained to Gordo and Lizzie.

Gordo's eyes were wide as he leaned toward Lizzie and whispered. "This guy really thinks he's one of Santa's helpers."

Lizzie nodded. The little old guy was cute . . . but something about him was definitely a little *off.* Still, Lizzie thought, he seems to be willing to help with the float. And let's face it, with Kate spending six thousand dollars on her Jingle Bug, I need all the help I can get.

CHAPTER TWO

"**H**ey, Lizzie—" Mr. McGuire called cheerfully as he, Matt, and Mrs. McGuire walked over to Lizzie's float, "I brought my power drill." He pulled the trigger button on the handle, making the motor give a loud *zzzing*!

"And I brought stuff to make paste," Matt said. "And my gum," he added, holding up a wrapped piece of Humongo Bubble.

I'm glad I put Matt in charge of the sticky stuff, Lizzie thought.

Lizzie's mom held out two plates. "And I made Christmas cookies," she said. "I got gingerbread Santas—" Then she smiled at Gordo and added, "And in honor of Hanukkah, I made potato pancakes." She held the plate out and Knobby the elf took it and passed it to Lizzie.

"Oh, thanks," Gordo said politely. He shuddered as Lizzie offered him the plate. "I can't get away from those," he whispered to Lizzie. "Every December, it's all I eat."

Lizzie giggled and put the plate down on the float trailer.

Knobby peered at Mrs. McGuire's plate of gingerbread Santas. "May I see one of the cookies?" he asked. Mrs. McGuire smiled and nodded, so Knobby pulled a Santa from the pile and grinned at it. "Oh, a very good likeness of him," Knobby said, nodding. "Of course, he has a scar on his neck from where he had a mole removed, but you can't expect a cookie to show that, huh?" Knobby chuckled.

Mrs. McGuire laughed.

"Had a tummy tuck also," Knobby went on.

Mr. and Mrs. McGuire gave each other a who-*is*-this-guy look.

"He's Santa's helper," Gordo explained.

"Oh, I'm sorry, I should have introduced myself—Knobby Frosty Bump." Knobby held out his hand, and Lizzie's dad shook it.

"Hi, Knobby," Mr. McGuire said, as though meeting a guy who thought he was an elf was the kind of thing he did every day of his life. "Sam McGuire."

"Oh, Sam McGuire—" Knobby frowned in thought. "You wanted a Kwik-E-Bake Oven when you were ten."

Everyone stared at Mr. McGuire. Gordo let out a snort of laughter.

"Uh. A lot of guys my age wanted those," Mr. McGuire said defensively. "To make pizza."

Lizzie had to struggle to keep from cracking up.

"Uh. I'm gonna go charge up my electric drill," Mr. McGuire said, giving the drill another *zzzing*. "This is a power tool," he went on, brandishing the drill as though it were a membership card to the Macho Men of the Universe Club. "Vrroom!"

Lizzie rolled her eyes as her dad scurried away.

"Santa's helper, huh?" Matt said, looking at Knobby skeptically. "Well, since I've got you here, I guess it'll save me a stamp—" Matt pulled out a piece of paper and unrolled it—all three feet of it. He handed the monster list to Knobby, who looked it over and frowned.

"Okay, so, I want three of those . . ." Matt said, pointing to the list. "The good kind of those . . . a brown one of those and the fish to feed it . . ."

"Sure," Knobby said, his gaze flickering from the list to Matt's face, "as long as you've been a good boy all year."

Matt looked at the list for a moment. "I'll just take that back, then," he said, plucking the list from Knobby's hand.

Lizzie sighed. She didn't have time for all of this—she needed to get to work on her float! "Okay," she said in a no-nonsense tone, "the first thing we're going to need to do is lay down a coat of burlap, so I'm going to need some paste." Lizzie looked at Matt.

"I'll go recharge my electronic organizer," Knobby said, looking distracted.

Gordo stared after the elf as he trotted away to find a free electrical outlet. "He may be a kook," Gordo said, "but he's a very friendly kook."

Matt picked up a green plastic bucket. "I'll go make it," he said, meaning the paste.

"Oh, I'll go help," Mrs. McGuire said, putting a hand on Matt's shoulder. "You remember the last time Matt was alone with paste," she said to Lizzie, then hurried after Matt.

Lizzie nodded. How could she forget? Matt had been covered in feathers for three days, and Lizzie's favorite pillow had never been the same.

Just then, Kate and Amy walked over. "If anyone comes to deliver a thirty-horsepower motor, send him to our float," Kate said, smiling evilly. "We're going to lunch."

Lizzie frowned as Kate and her friend strutted away. She couldn't believe this! Okay, forget the fact that Kate hadn't even been there for five minutes and was already going to lunch. That part was easy to believe. No, Lizzie had bigger problems.

"Their float's gonna have a motor?" she wailed. Then she gritted her teeth and turned to Gordo. "Look," Lizzie said. "I am going to beat Kate, and I am going to win first place in this thing. And you and my family are going to help me."

Just then, Matt, Knobby, and Mr. and Mrs. McGuire came trooping back. Matt was carrying a bucket of paste, and Mr. and Mrs. McGuire were laughing at some joke Knobby had just told. Probably about Rudolph or Mrs. Claus, Lizzie thought. This guy's act was starting to get on her nerves.

"That's a good one, Knobby!" Mr. McGuire said. "So, uh, Lizzie, we're out of here."

Lizzie's eyes grew round.

"We're going to have lunch with Knobby," Mrs. McGuire said brightly. She chuckled. "He has the most incredible stories."

"And he knows a great Chinese place," Matt said eagerly.

"*Dui, dui. Mei yo chien. Tsai jen,*" Knobby said.

Okay, Lizzie thought. I guess that was Chinese. Or else this guy is really crazy.

She glanced at her family. They were grinning like fools, clearly impressed with their new elf friend.

"You want to come with us?" Mrs. McGuire asked Lizzie.

"No," Lizzie snapped, frowning. "I have to work on my float, *remember*?" She looked at her pile of raw materials meaningfully.

"Okay, Lizzie," her dad said, totally oblivious to her message. "Well, look, we'll be back soon. Come on, Knobby."

Matt handed the green plastic bucket full of goo to Lizzie. "Here's the paste—" he said. "We'll see you later."

The McGuires—minus Lizzie, but plus Knobby—headed off for lunch.

Lizzie frowned down at her paste. That was it? Her family had come to help her, and all they did was mix up some goop and then leave for lunch? How was Rock 'n' Roll Xmas ever going to happen?

And we're off to a great start.

Much, much later, Lizzie walked into her house, grimy and scowling. "I'm home!" she called. "I hope you enjoyed your six-hour lunch because I got, like, *nothing* finished on the float!"

No answer. Lizzie walked into the living room and saw a grown man in red-and-white-striped tights and a green outfit shaking the presents under the Christmas tree.

Lizzie screamed.

Knobby jumped and let out a yell. Recovering, he quickly put the toy down. "Oh," he said. "I was just checking your toys. If there's one thing that fascinates me, it's toy quality. Toys and Latin dancing," Knobby added. He did a wiggly little dance move. "Cha-cha-cha—"

"*You* . . . what are you doing in my house?" Lizzie asked, totally freaked out.

Knobby gestured to his outrageous elf outfit. It was an even more elaborate costume than the one he had worn at the Cheer-ity Drive that afternoon. "Well," Knobby said, "your brother wanted to see my work duds, so we swung by the retirement hotel where I live. We were having so much fun, we lost track of time. Your parents even asked me to dinner."

He grinned. "We're having spaghetti!"

Matt ran into the living room, carrying a mug of steaming cocoa. "Knobby, Knobby—here's your hot chocolate!" He handed the mug to the elf man.

"Oh, thank you, Mattie," Knobby said, taking the cocoa. "But it might not make a difference about your present." He lifted his eyebrows. "Your own Caribbean island is kind of a tall order."

"Well," Matt said, handing Knobby a dollar, "see what you can do."

Lizzie couldn't believe her eyes. "Well, how about what *I* want for Christmas?" Lizzie demanded, folding her arms across her chest. "I want to get my float finished."

"You don't have to listen to her, Knobby," Matt said. "She's a Grinch—only the Grinch smells better."

Knobby laughed.

"I do not hate Christmas," Lizzie insisted. "I love Christmas. I love everything about Christmas. And I love having Santa's helper in my house." She forced herself to smile. "I think it's simply charming."

I am a positive person, Lizzie told herself. I *will* look on the bright side of having Knobby around—even if it kills me.

"Well, that's good," Mrs. McGuire said as she and her husband walked into the living room. "Because Knobby's going to be staying with us for a few days."

Matt clapped eagerly.

Lizzie noticed that her mom was holding yet another plate of Christmas cookies. Just how many of those things did she bake? Lizzie wondered.

"Yeah, the plumbing's busted in his retirement home, so he's got nowhere to stay till it's fixed," Mr. McGuire added.

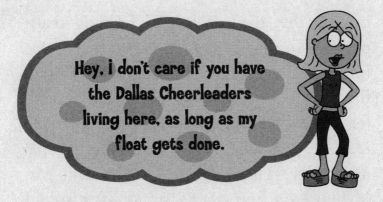

Hey, I don't care if you have the Dallas Cheerleaders living here, as long as my float gets done.

Lizzie's new positive attitude about Knobby didn't last long, though. For one thing, when they sat down to dinner, Knobby scooped all of the spaghetti from the platter onto his plate before Lizzie had taken her first helping.

Lizzie was about to protest, but her mom flashed her a warning look, so instead Lizzie had to fill up on the Brussels sprouts. *Yum-yum.*

After dinner, Lizzie tried to convince her family to go back to the warehouse with her and do a little work on the float, but Knobby insisted that they sit by the fire and make popcorn strands for the Christmas tree. Lizzie had to bite her lip to keep from screaming in frustration. The tree was already decorated, for Pete's sake! But Matt was psyched at the idea of popcorn, so he put some in the microwave. Then Lizzie, Knobby, and Mr. McGuire sat and strung strand after strand while Matt sat eating the kernels at the end of the string.

Meanwhile, Mrs. McGuire had announced that they would have fruitcake for dessert. Mrs. Neumann from down the street had given one to the McGuires as a home-baked holiday present.

Lizzie's mom went to the kitchen and got out the big knife. There was only one problem—the fruitcake had the consistency of a cement block. Normal cutting tools had no effect on it. After twenty minutes, Mrs.

McGuire had to give up. She went to get her husband, who was busy arranging the Nativity scene with two Wise Men and one X-Man. (One of the Wise Men had mysteriously disappeared two years ago, around the time that Matt had gotten a new set of Legos and declared that he wanted to build a Lego car and needed an action figure that was small enough to drive it.)

Mr. McGuire followed his wife into the kitchen and threw all of his muscle behind cutting the cake. No good. Finally, Mr. McGuire got so mad that he picked up the singing Santa that sat on the kitchen island and used it to smash the fruitcake. Not a single crumb came loose. They even tried a hammer and chisel—useless. Finally, Mrs. McGuire gave up and served everyone peppermint ice cream with hot fudge on it. Everyone seemed very relieved.

But the worst part of the whole evening, as far as Lizzie was concerned, was the mistletoe her dad hung up. Mr. McGuire put up little clusters of mistletoe all along the entryway between the kitchen and the living room, and insisted that Mrs. McGuire stop and give him a kiss at each one. Gross, Lizzie thought as she watched her mom laugh and give her dad another peck on the lips. Who wants to watch their parents kissing?

Knobby and Matt spent about an hour playing with a dreidel. Lizzie had to admit that she'd never seen anyone play as well as Knobby did. He won all of Matt's gold-wrapped chocolate coins! Knobby grinned as he swept the edible money over to his side of the table, then offered to loan Matt a few, so they could go double or nothing.

Finally, Knobby suggested that they gather around the piano to sing a few carols. They had made it through "Winter Wonderland" and "Hark the Herald Angels Sing," when Knobby suggested Lizzie's least favorite carol of all—"The Twelve Days of Christmas." Lizzie sighed. Matt always drew out the song as long as possible, warbling all the notes like a hound dog at the Grand Ol' Opry. But Lizzie didn't dare to complain. She knew that her parents would be all over her if she did.

Knobby suggested that they each sing a different line, and Lizzie sighed again. Now Matt would really go crazy.

"Eight maids a-milking," Matt chirped.

"Seven swans a-swimming," Mrs. McGuire sang.

"Six geese a-laying," Lizzie added, as enthusiastically as she could manage, considering she knew what was coming next.

Matt closed his eyes, and began his crazy warbling. "Five golden . . ."—he took a big breath so that he could really belt out the word, "rings"—but just then, the electronic tinkling of "Jingle Bells" sounded from Knobby's pocket.

The senior citizen elf pulled out his cell phone. "Sorry," he said, wincing apologetically. "I have to take this." He turned his attention to the receiver. "Frosty Bump here, talk to me. . . . Yeah, yeah," he nodded; then his expression changed. "We can't get it done by Christmas?" Knobby sounded really upset. "So many people will be disappointed. . . ."

Lizzie folded her arms across her chest as Knobby hung up. "What?" she demanded. "Another one of your elves? Can't get the toys done in time?"

Knobby shook his head. "Augie Basmajian Plumbing and Heating," he explained. "They can't get the pipes fixed by Christmas."

"Why not?" Mrs. McGuire asked.

Knobby shrugged. "No workers. Everybody's taking the holidays off."

"But the toys are okay, right?" Matt asked. Matt actually looks worried, Lizzie thought. I can't believe my family is buying all of this elf stuff!

"Oh, the toys'll be there on Christmas," Knobby reassured Matt. "Don't worry about that."

But that still didn't solve Knobby's problem. What would he and his friends do without a place to take a shower in for a week? The McGuires looked at one another.

"I can do the plumbing," Mr. McGuire suddenly said, standing up from his place at the piano bench.

Everyone stared at him doubtfully.

"I've got the tools," Lizzie's dad went on, "I've taken a couple of courses. We can get it done in a couple of days."

"I'll help," Matt said.

Mrs. McGuire nodded. "Count me in."

Lizzie's dad grinned. "Yeah."

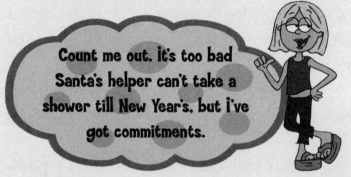

Count me out. It's too bad Santa's helper can't take a shower till New Year's, but i've got commitments.

Lizzie pouted. "But what about my Rock 'n' Roll Christmas float?" she asked. "I need help to finish it!"

"Well, you and Gordo can work on it together, can't you?" Mrs. McGuire suggested.

Lizzie shrugged and looked at the floor. "I guess."

Lizzie looked around at her family. She really couldn't believe that they were deserting her at a time like this!

Oh, well, Lizzie thought. I guess a girl's gotta do what a girl's gotta do.

And what I've gotta do is make a couple of fake trees, some reindeer out of chicken wire, and a giant cottage for Santa, with only Gordo to help me. No problem.

This could still be the best Christmas ever.

Yeah, right.

CHAPTER THREE

Lizzie scowled at the pile of boards and stacks of newspaper that sat on her trailer. She and Gordo had worked all day yesterday, and it looked like they hadn't accomplished a thing! Now they were back, no doubt for another day of endless frustration.

Just then, Larry walked over. He was carrying a fog gun, and spraying gray mist everywhere. "Hey, guys—you seen the smoke machine I got for my float?" he asked, shooting out more fog. "This is gonna make all the X-wings crashing into the Death Star seem really authentic."

"Right," Gordo said eyeing the smoke machine, "because nothing says Merry Christmas like a fiery spaceship crash."

Larry let out a freaky-sounding sarcastic laugh, then walked away, happily spraying smoke through the whole warehouse.

Lizzie threw up her hands in frustration. "He's got special effects!" she griped. "Kate's got pros building her float!" She peered at her float sketches. "I've gotta make this bigger. . . ." she muttered.

it'll be a lot of work, but i can still grind everyone else into the dust. in the spirit of the holidays.

"Hey, Lizzie," Mr. McGuire said as he walked over to Lizzie's pile of supplies. "How's the float coming along?"

Lizzie forced herself to seem cheerful. "It's good," she lied. "It's going to take us all day to finish," she said, nodding at Gordo, "but I think we can do it. Did you guys finish the plumbing?" she asked hopefully.

Lizzie's dad shook his head. "Not exactly. It's taking a little longer than we had hoped."

I'll bet, Lizzie thought. She could just imagine her family standing in the basement of Knobby's retirement home, getting doused with dirty water from a bunch of broken pipes.

"I just came by to pick up some hacksaw blades from my toolbox," Mr. McGuire went on.

"Do you guys think you'll finish in time?" Gordo asked.

Mr. McGuire shook his head. "I don't know. I don't really think we have enough help. What I'm afraid of is that Knobby and his friends won't have any place to stay for Christmas."

"Well, is there anything I can do to help?" Gordo asked.

Lizzie stared at him. Was her friend really saying what she thought he was saying?

"Sure," Lizzie's dad said, "we can always use an extra pair of hands."

"Cool." Gordo put down the chicken wire he had been unrolling and started to follow Mr. McGuire out of the warehouse.

Lizzie couldn't believe Gordo was totally ditching her! "But, what about my float, Gordo?" she demanded.

"I'm sorry, Lizzie," Gordo said, "it's just— well, I think fixing plumbing is a little more important."

"But . . ." Lizzie stared at her pile of supplies, her dreams of Aspen disappearing like the gray smog from Larry's smoke machine. "What about my float?"

"Lizzie," said Gordo, "would you want to go a week without a bath?" He rolled his eyes. "No."

"Sorry, Lizzie," Mr. McGuire added. "Listen, if we get done early, we'll come back and help you out," he added brightly.

Lizzie frowned as they left. Right, she thought, like there's any way that my parents, Gordo, and Matt are going to get finished fixing plumbing early . . . or ever.

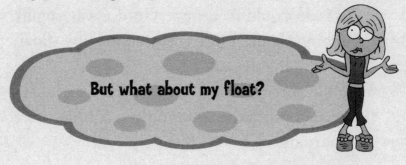

But what about my float?

CHAPTER FOUR

Okay, Lizzie decided—as they say, if you want something done right, you just have to do it yourself. She rubbed her hands together and looked at her sketches again. I can totally do this, she told herself. It'll be easy. I'll just start with the hardest thing first.

Lizzie grabbed a roll of chicken wire. She unwrapped a section and tried to bend it into a shape. She had seen someone on a home-decorating show do this. "Chicken-wire reindeer,"

Lizzie said to herself as she wrestled with the tough wire. "Chicken-wire reindeer. Chicken-wire reindeer. Chicken-wire—ow!" The chicken wire had attacked her finger! Lizzie stuck her finger in her mouth and glared at the wire. Okay, she decided, so maybe starting with the hardest stuff first wasn't the best idea. . . .

Lizzie fished a Band-Aid out of her purse and bandaged her finger. Time to try something else. Gordo had actually made some progress on his Christmas tree the day before, so Lizzie took that over. Gordo had painted some cardboard brown and green, so Lizzie cut it out into a shape that more or less resembled a Christmas tree, then tried to figure out a way to make it stand up on its own. She tried a zillion different ways, but nothing worked. After an hour and a half, Lizzie finally gave up. Maybe I can just hold it up during the parade, she mused. Or maybe I can just buy a fake Christmas tree.

After another couple of hours spent in an attempt to paste the burlap onto the platform, Lizzie sank down to the floor, exhausted. It was almost nine o'clock, and her float still looked horrible. The Christmas parade is tomorrow, and my float is nothing but a hunk of chicken wire and a pile of crumpled newspaper, Lizzie thought miserably.

But she still wouldn't give up. Maybe I can at least make it look a little pretty, she thought deliriously. She painted some paste in the shape of stars onto the side of a box and thrust her hand into a bag of glitter. "Pretty glitter," Lizzie said, exhausted, as she tossed the glitter at the box. "Pretty glitter."

She imagined her family and Gordo fixing the pipes at Knobby's retirement hotel. They're probably singing Christmas carols,

Lizzie thought bitterly—while I'm here trying to work magic with a handful of glitter. She stared at the box, bleary-eyed. This was definitely not working.

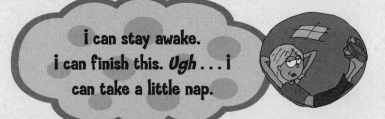

i can stay awake. i can finish this. *Ugh* . . . i can take a little nap.

Lizzie was getting really sleepy. All I need is a little rest, she thought as she curled up on a pile of supplies and laid her head down. "Pretty glitter," she mumbled.

Just then, a gentle gust of wind blew across Lizzie's face. Lizzie's eyes fluttered open, and she saw Knobby leaning over her, shaking her shoulder. He was wearing an elf costume that was even more elaborate than anything Lizzie had seen yet. And the most amazing thing was happening . . . it was snowing inside the warehouse!

"Lizzie," Knobby said gently. "Lizzie—wake up."

"Knobby?" Lizzie asked groggily. "What are you doing here?"

"I'm Santa's helper," Knobby said seriously. "And I'm worried about a young lady who has lost sight of what Christmas is all about."

"What?" Lizzie asked slowly. "Are you talking about *me*?"

Knobby nodded at the pile of crumpled newspapers that were lying beneath Lizzie's trailer. "I'm not talking about the pile of trash in the corner, there," he said sternly.

"Hey," Lizzie said with a frown, "that's my float."

"It is?" Knobby said. "Oh . . . yes. Very nice. Good job. Oh, yes."

Lizzie rolled her eyes. "And I have not lost

sight of what Christmas is about," she insisted.

"Well, I have someone here who thinks you're wrong," Knobby said. He helped Lizzie to her feet. "Say hello to the Elf Who Wants to Be a Dentist—" Knobby waved, and Lizzie gaped as Gordo walked out, dressed as an elf . . . and carrying a giant tooth!

Wait a minute, Lizzie thought. Wasn't the elf who wanted to be a dentist a character on the *Rudolph the Red-Nosed Reindeer* special? Why is Gordo dressed up as him?

"I didn't want to make toys," elf Gordo said in a weird, chirpy voice. "I wanted to be a dentist, so I could help people. 'Cause helping people's what it's all about."

"Well, I wish people would help me finish my float," Lizzie said testily. She was still kind of mad at Gordo . . . even if he had become an elf.

"Why are you so obsessed with this float, Lizzie McGuire?" Gordo asked innocently. "Why?" Then, without waiting for a response, Gordo walked away cheerfully, even kicking his heels in the air.

"Here with the answer to that," Knobby said, "is the Ghost of Christmas Past."

Mrs. McGuire appeared. She was wearing a red velvet Victorian-style blouse over a long green silk skirt. Her blond hair was styled in ringlets, over which she wore a bonnet. Why is everyone turning into people from holiday TV? Lizzie wondered. Her mom's outfit was straight out of *A Christmas Carol.*

"Okay," Lizzie said impatiently. "This is crazy. Junk food must be giving me a bad dream or something." She frowned at her mother. "Mom, you're not the Ghost of Christmas Past—you're the pepperoni pizza that I ate for dinner!"

"Lizzie," Mrs. McGuire said, "could pepperoni do this?" Suddenly, Mrs. McGuire grew fifteen feet tall, then she shrank back to her normal height.

"Okay," said Lizzie, buying it for the moment, "what do you want to show me, Spirit?"

"Look, Lizzie," Mrs. McGuire said, pointing. "Look at the TV box."

Lizzie glanced over at the TV box. Instead of glitter stars, Lizzie saw her bedroom. It was in its usual state—a total mess. Clothes were strewn everywhere, along with magazines, fast-food wrappers, CD cases, and various kinds of cosmetics.

"It's my bedroom," Lizzie said. "Why are you showing me my room?"

"Because it's a mess!" Mrs. McGuire barked. "Would it kill you to clean it up once in a while?"

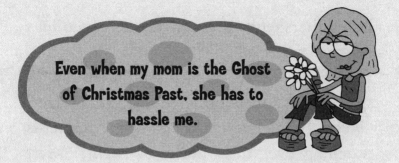

Even when my mom is the Ghost of Christmas Past, she has to hassle me.

"The point is," Mrs. McGuire said, "instead of enjoying Christmas with the rest of us, you're obsessed with winning."

"Okay, so maybe Christmas isn't about my float," Lizzie admitted. "But I'm getting a little confused." She glanced at Knobby. "What *is* it about?"

Suddenly, Lizzie heard a familiar voice. "I'll tell you what Christmas is really about, Lizzie McGuire."

Lizzie looked over and saw Matt, dressed in a blue-and-white-striped T-shirt. He also had a light blue blanket draped over his head, à la

Linus the shepherd from the *Charlie Brown Christmas Special.*

"Lights, please," Matt said solemnly. A spotlight snapped on, lighting up his face. "Near Bethlehem, there were shepherds watching over their flocks by night," Matt said. "And then the angel of the Lord appeared before them. 'Fear not,' said the angel, 'for I bring you tidings of great joy. For unto you is born this day, in the city of David, a child who shall be your Savior.' And suddenly, the angel was surrounded by a great multitude of the heavenly host, singing 'Glory to God in the highest, and on earth peace and goodwill toward men. . . .'" Matt looked at Lizzie. "And that's the real meaning of Christmas, Lizzie McGuire." Matt pulled the blanket from his head and walked away.

Suddenly, Mr. McGuire jogged up to Lizzie and Knobby. "You know, I do a really great

Wise Man," he said. A giant net fell over his head and dragged him away. "Hey, hey, hey!"

Lizzie pressed her lips together, thinking hard. "I shouldn't care about winning something for myself," she said slowly, shaking her head. "I mean, Christmas is about doing good for others. Just like all you guys, fixing the plumbing." She looked up at Knobby. "By the way, I hope that's going okay."

"I can show you how it's going," Knobby said.

Suddenly, a new image appeared on the side of the TV box. It was Lizzie's family, in the basement of the retirement hotel. Lizzie's parents, Matt, and Gordo were all adjusting the pipes, humming Christmas carols as they worked.

Suddenly, Lizzie felt like a character in a Christmas special, too—she felt like the Grinch! Her heart had definitely been two sizes two small. But just like the Grinch, her heart instantly grew. As Lizzie watched her family and Gordo work, a patter of Dr. Seuss-ish rhymes bubbled out of her:

"They're dirty and grimy.
Their hands must be stinging.
But yet they keep plumbing.
They're plumbing and singing!
But how can they plumb,
when they plumb without tools?
They plumb without skipples,
dee-daddles, or zools!"

Then the image of the singing plumbers disappeared. Lizzie sighed. "No wonder they make no plumb progress at all, because the pipes that they're plumbing are two sizes too small."

Lizzie blinked. She suddenly knew what to

do! "I could still help them!" she cried. "And we could get finished in time! I just have to get over there."

"Lizzie," Knobby said as he smiled at her, "you've had the power to go there all along."

"I know," Lizzie said. "I just close my eyes and click my heels three times."

Knobby looked confused. "Why would you do that? I've got my Olds Delta 88 parked outside. I'll give you a lift."

Suddenly, Knobby disappeared.

That was when Lizzie woke up. She looked around, blinking, then struggled to stand up. She had just realized something important. "Santa's helper drives a gas-guzzler!" she cried. No, wait—that wasn't the important thing. Lizzie shook her head, to clear it. Right—the retirement hotel. "I've gotta get over there. I hope I'm not too late!"

CHAPTER FIVE

Mrs. McGuire let out a sigh. She and Matt had been watching Gordo and Mr. McGuire trying to fit a pipe into a joint. But it just wouldn't fit! They had been working on these pipes for hours with no luck. Now it was looking like they might not be able to fix the pipes in time for Christmas, after all!

The only person who didn't seem down about the pipes was Knobby. He was sleeping in the corner.

Mr. McGuire tried again with the pipe. "Aggh!" He shook his head. "It's no use, there's just no way it's going to fit." He gestured to the pipes with his wrench. "There's no way we're going to get this done in time."

"The old folks won't have anywhere to spend Christmas," Gordo said. He shook his head. "Bummer."

"Can't they stay with us?" Matt suggested. "They can share my room."

"Oh, honey," Mrs. McGuire said. Her voice sounded exhausted. "There are two hundred and forty of them."

Matt shrugged. "They can share Lizzie's room, too." He grinned.

Mrs. McGuire laughed.

"Matt," Mr. McGuire warned.

"Uh, no," said a voice behind them. "I don't think so. I'm not sharing my room—"

The McGuires and Gordo turned to see Lizzie striding into the room.

"Because we're going to get this finished tonight," Lizzie added. She grinned.

"What about your float?" Gordo asked. "It won't get done in time."

"Yeah," said Mr. McGuire.

"I know," Lizzie admitted, "but I shouldn't care about my float winning first prize. What matters is finding pipes the right size."

Everyone stared at Lizzie for a minute. Since when did she talk in rhyming couplets?

"Okay," Lizzie said. She looked at the plumbing and assessed the situation. "We need to change out the main line and use stepped-down couplings."

"Wow," Mr. McGuire said, "how did you think of that, Lizzie? That could work!"

Lizzie smiled, remembering her dream. "I

don't know," she said with a shrug. "It just kind of . . . came to me."

"Well, however it came to you, young lady, you have just saved the day," Mr. McGuire said happily.

"Well, that's what Christmas is about," Lizzie said. "It shouldn't be about my float having reindeer, or candy canes on it. It should be . . ." she looked around the dirty basement, at her grimy-faced family, and at her friend who had spent hours helping out an old elf he didn't even know. "It should be about this," Lizzie finished.

Matt looked confused. "What—hot water for Santa's helper?"

"No—" Lizzie said, shaking her head, "*helping people*. And I would never have realized that if it weren't for Knobby." She looked toward the corner, where Knobby had been sleeping. He had disappeared!

"Where did Knobby go?" Mrs. McGuire asked.

"Hello, people," Matt said in his best *Duh!* voice, "Uh. Christmas Eve? Santa's helper? Where do you *think* he went?"

Everyone looked at one another. Even Lizzie had to draw in her breath. Could it really be true? Could Knobby really be Santa's chief elf, after all? Whatever the explanation, it was a totally way-out, genuine-type magical moment.

"Hey, everybody." Knobby walked into the basement, drying his hands on a paper towel. "I had to go down to the little boys' room in the gas station."

Okay, Lizzie thought, maybe it wasn't such a magical moment.

"What?" Knobby asked. Everyone was staring at him as if he'd just turned into a reindeer. He gestured to the pipes. "The plumbing's busted here."

Lizzie had to smile as everyone got back to

work. It all felt just right now, the plumbing and singing, while outside, Christmas bells had just started ringing!

The next day was Christmas, and Lizzie's whole family had left the house early to meet Gordo at the Christmas parade. The sun was out, the sky was blue, and Lizzie couldn't wait to get back home and open her presents. Still, it was fun to see all the floats. Everyone had worked so hard this year.

Larry's Death Star Christmas looked pretty good, actually. Weird, but good. Lizzie was only a little bummed that Rock 'n' Roll Xmas wouldn't be making an appearance. She was still sure that she could have won that Aspen trip.

"And now, the Wendell Wilkie High School marching band," the parade grand marshal announced, "performing 'Carol of the Bells.' It's one of my favorites."

The high school band from across town burst into the familiar music. Wearing their snazzy red uniforms, the band fit right in with the spirit of the season.

Mrs. McGuire gave her daughter's arm a little squeeze. "Honey, I'm so proud of you, giving up working on your float to help us out."

Lizzie shrugged. "It was fun," she said, and she meant it. Sure, her float could have been cool. But knowing that a couple of hundred older people could go back to their home, thanks to what her family and Gordo had done, felt great.

Just then, Kate's cousin Amy walked up to Lizzie and smiled smugly.

"We dropped by the warehouse last night," Amy said snidely. "Saw your float. Why isn't it out by the trash cans?"

"Merry Christmas to you, too, Amy," Lizzie replied.

Just then, Kate strutted over to join them.

Great, Lizzie thought, more Christmas joy.

"Oh, my gosh," Kate gushed. She gave her hair a toss and smiled meanly at Lizzie. "I can't wait to see your face when *my* float comes down the street."

The grand marshal piped up again to announce the next float. "And the theme is: 'The Splendor of Christmas' by Reginald Reehoven and Alistair Stuccovich."

"Hey, look—" Mr. McGuire said, pointing. "That's my cousin Ree-Ree and his buddy Stucco." He held up his video camera to capture the moment.

Stucco was wearing plastic reindeer antlers and a red Rudolph nose, and pulling Ree-Ree on a wagon behind him. Ree-Ree had on a Santa cap that had definitely seen better days, and was tossing some kind of treats into the crowd.

"The Splendor of Christmas seems to be a

disoriented moose hauling some form of dock worker," the grand marshal announced. "At any rate, they're pelting the crowd with double-A batteries."

"Ow!" cried a woman as she was struck by a handful of the treats.

"Incoming!" Matt cried as a fistful of batteries flew their way. "Duck and cover!"

"Oh! I've just been informed the batteries are for children's toys," the grand marshal announced. "How nice." He flinched as a battery beaned him in the face.

Another wayward battery nearly knocked Larry Tudgeman out cold.

Luckily, Lizzie and her family ducked in time, and the batteries whizzed overhead. Lizzie smiled. No double-A batteries were going to ruin this day.

"The plumbing got fixed, and Knobby and his friends have a place to stay," she said. "I'd say 'Best Christmas Ever' definitely applies."

"That's the spirit," said a voice behind her.

Lizzie turned around and saw the cool-looking Santa from the Cheer-ity Drive. Knobby was standing beside him.

"Hey," Lizzie said to Santa with a smile, "it's you."

"I thought you'd like to meet the head honcho," Knobby said. "But he doesn't have much time. He has to be at a meeting in Korea in three and a half hours."

"I heard what you did for Knobby," Santa said to Lizzie. "Righteous."

Gordo leaned toward Lizzie, clearly amused. "Santa just said 'righteous.'"

Lizzie ignored her friend. "Well, I was glad to help," she told Santa.

A crowd of kids gathered around Santa. One little girl looked up at him and frowned. "Are you *really* Santa?" she asked.

"Well, I ain't the Easter Bunny," Santa replied.

"You're too skinny to be Santa," a little boy said.

"Hey," Santa protested, "I'm working on it."

"Well, you may be too skinny," an older girl said sarcastically, "but you sure look old enough."

"Hey!" Santa cried.

"If you're Santa, prove it," a blond boy demanded.

"Yeah, prove it," another little boy agreed.

Santa growled. "Take a hike, you little. . . ."

"No, Santa," Knobby put a hand on Santa's arm and shook his head. "Santa."

"All right," Santa grumbled, "I'll prove it, but only because I like showing off."

There was a slight shriek of feedback as the grand marshal announced the next float.

"And now, ladies and gentlemen, the next float. Rock 'n' Roll Christmas by Lizzie McGuire."

Lizzie gaped in disbelief. "What?!" she cried. "No. My float is a hunk of chicken wire and a box. I didn't get to finish it."

Gordo shrugged. "Well, *somebody* did."

Lizzie was speechless—her float was amazing! It looked even better than she had imagined it—a classic 1960s convertible pulled a spectacular Christmas scene with six full-sized decorated trees, glistening under a layer of sparkly snow. The giant candy canes and penguins looked adorable placed around the entrance to a life-sized reproduction of Santa's workshop. And out in front, behind a microphone decorated with a glittery red-and-white feather boa, was a cool-looking rock singer.

"And I think I know who made this happen," Lizzie said.

"I think you do know, Lizzie," Knobby replied.

The singer burst into a seriously rocking rendition of "Santa Claus Is Coming to Town." The crowd was on its feet instantly, clapping and cheering like mad. Lizzie's float was better than a rock concert—and about three times as loud!

Gordo shook his head. "So, you're saying that Santa Claus finished your float, complete with a live rock singer to perform on it. I did not see that one coming."

Lizzie laughed. What could she say? Neither did she. But one look at Kate's shocked face gave Lizzie a warm, holiday feeling inside.

No doubt about it—this was definitely the best Christmas ever.

Lizzie
McGUIRE

PART
TWO

CHAPTER ONE

"**G**uys! Guys! Guys!" Lizzie shouted—she had major news that she had to tell her best friends Miranda and Gordo right away. Lizzie burst through the cafeteria double doors, still shouting. Unfortunately, she whacked a kid with the door, and his lunch tray went flying—all over Lizzie.

And Lizzie landed flat on her face.

At my age, you'd think i could run and talk at the same time.

Way to ruin the biggest news since the invention of deodorant, Lizzie thought as she struggled to her feet. *Ugh.* She was covered in macaroni and cheese . . . and the macaroni and cheese at Hillridge Junior High had a seriously funky smell, kind of like an old sponge.

Miranda and Gordo stared at Lizzie from their seats at their usual table.

"Forget lunch!" Lizzie commanded as she hauled herself to her feet. "Forget eating!"

Miranda gave Lizzie one of those looks. You know, that has-all-that-hair-spray-finally-affected-your-brain? look. Lizzie knew it well. "The cafeteria food's not *that* bad," Miranda teased.

"You know, you can save the stuff on your shirt for later," Gordo suggested.

Lizzie looked down at her shirt and picked off a couple of clinging macaroni piecess. How can my friends think about food at a time like this? she wondered as she slid into the seat opposite Gordo. "Forget that," Lizzie gasped. "Zander. Knight." Lizzie flapped her hand in excitement. "Coming. Here."

Miranda's eyes went wide.

"Are you speaking in code?" Gordo asked, frowning.

"Explain yourself," Miranda commanded, lifting her eyebrows so high that they completely disappeared beneath her dark bangs. "Pronto."

"Zander-Knight-is-coming-here-to-shoot-his-new-music-video-Christmas-special," Lizzie blurted in one long breath. Now that she had actually said it out loud, she felt light-headed.

Of course, she could also be feeling that way from talking so fast she didn't have time to breathe! Zander Knight, she thought dizzily. Zander Knight is coming here!

I'm goin' to Zander's party!

"This better not be a joke," Miranda said. Her dark eyes flashed, and her voice was deadly serious.

"It's not a joke," Lizzie insisted. "His holiday video shoots tomorrow."

Gordo looked at Lizzie. "So who's Zander Knight?"

Lizzie gaped at her friend. Honestly, Lizzie thought, sometimes I wonder how Gordo can be so smart and so clueless at the same time.

Miranda ignored him. "So," she asked Lizzie, "where's it gonna be?"

Lizzie pressed her lips together. "I don't know," she admitted. "It's a secret. But we're gonna find out."

Gordo looked around casually. "I bet it

would be real helpful to ask a guy who knows about films to figure out where they'd shoot the video," he said.

"Where?" Lizzie asked eagerly.

Miranda rolled her eyes, as though she didn't believe that a guy who had no clue who Zander Knight was might actually be able to guess where the star's video might be shooting. "Where?" she challenged.

Gordo nodded. "First you back up and tell me who this Zander Knight is."

"Okay," Lizzie said eagerly, "he's a singer, a dancer, a movie star—"

"And he's our age!" Miranda added, clapping her hands in excitement.

Gordo thought for a moment. "So this would probably be a lot more exciting if I were a teenage girl."

Lizzie and Miranda looked at each other and nodded.

"So, where do you think it shoots?" Lizzie asked, leaning forward in her chair. *Now that we've given* Clueless *Gordo the 411, it's time to put* Smart *Gordo to work.*

"I don't know," Gordo said with a shrug. "But I bet it won't be that difficult to figure it out."

"I could interview Zander Knight for the school WebZine!" Lizzie said. She was so excited, she half-expected smoke to start pouring out of her ears. "I've already got my press badge from Mr. Lang. That should get us in."

"I am so there," Miranda said. "Maybe I could sing for him."

Lizzie nodded. Miranda had a terrific voice—singing for Zander Knight could be a huge break for her!

"It'd be pretty cool to go to a real set," Gordo said, half to himself. "Hey, I could do

one of those behind-the-scenes documen-
taries," he added, pointing at Lizzie. "They
kill at the major film festivals. I'm in."

Lizzie grinned. "So all we have to do is figure out where it shoots."

"And how to get in," Miranda added.

"And how to meet him," Lizzie went on.
Gordo shrugged. "No problem."

Tomorrow, i have a date with
destiny. . . .
What am i gonna wear?!

"So, Gordo, what's the game plan?" Lizzie
asked.

After school, Lizzie, Miranda, and Gordo
had gone over to Lizzie's house. Now they

were sitting on Lizzie's bed, searching through a pile of phone books.

Gordo bit his lip and frowned at the map of the town he'd tacked to Lizzie's closet door. "Well," he said, "a video shoot needs lots of space. So it's got to be somewhere big— enough room for the crew, the equipment, and, of course, the set."

"And Zander," Miranda added quickly. "Can't forget Zander."

"What about the mall?" Lizzie suggested. "The mall's big."

"Popular choice for an up-and-coming singer." Gordo nodded and slapped a red-tape *X* onto the map where the mall was located.

Lizzie smiled and jotted a note on a pad of paper, feeling like a genius. This is going to be a piece of cake, she thought. In just five seconds, they had already come up with a good lead.

This is a cinch. I can snoop out secret video shoots in my sleep.

"Hey kids," Mrs. McGuire said as she poked her head into Lizzie's room.

"Hey, Mom," Lizzie said.

"Hey, Mrs. McGuire," Miranda said.

Gordo gave Lizzie's mom a little wave. "Hi."

"Lizzie, your dad's working late tonight, so I thought I'd order a pizza," Mrs. McGuire said.

"Sweet." Lizzie smiled. "Extra cheese, please."

Lizzie's mom nodded. "Okay. You guys gonna stay for dinner?" she asked Miranda and Gordo.

Gordo grinned. "Mrs. McGuire, have we ever turned down a free meal?"

"I'll take that as a yes," Mrs. McGuire replied. She smiled and closed the door gently.

Lizzie grinned after her. A lead for the Zander Knight video shoot *and* extra-cheese pizza, she thought. This day just keeps getting better and better!

This day just keeps getting worse and worse, Lizzie thought three hours later. She glanced up at the map, which was now covered in red *X*s. She and her friends had called almost every major event space in Hillridge, posing as Zander Knight's agent. But no one knew anything about a video shoot.

Lizzie stared down at the nearly empty pizza box. There were only two slices left. She, Miranda, and Gordo had torn through most of the pizza half an hour ago. Scoping out video locations is hungry work, Lizzie thought.

Gordo clicked off the phone and shook his head. "I've called everywhere," he said with a sigh. "I have no idea where the shoot is," he finally admitted.

"I thought you said this was gonna be easy to figure out," Miranda griped.

Gordo shrugged. "I was wrong."

Just then, Matt wandered into Lizzie's room and grabbed a slice of pizza.

"Well, how do we know that this Zander Knight thing isn't a hoax?" Gordo blurted out. "Like that rumor that the school cafeteria serves squirrel?"

"It's no lie," Matt said confidently.

For a second, Lizzie nearly gagged, thinking that her brother was talking about the squirrel-meat rumor. Then she realized that he meant the Zander Knight story, and frowned. Why did Matt always claim to know everything?

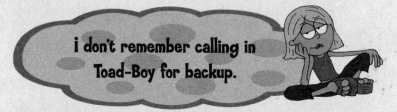

i don't remember calling in Toad-Boy for backup.

Lizzie hauled the phone books off her lap and stood up. "I thought the deal was that you could come in my room on the condition that you didn't speak," she said to her brother.

Matt ignored her and glanced over at the *X*-filled map. "Not even close," he muttered, shaking his head.

"Oh, and how would you know?" Lizzie scoffed.

"Lanny told me," Matt replied.

Lizzie looked at Gordo and Miranda. Gordo gave a gesture, and the three of them huddled up." So, what'dya guys think?" he asked in a low voice.

"I think he's telling the truth," Lizzie said.

"How do we get him to tell us?" Miranda asked.

"Well, we gotta give him something," Lizzie suggested.

"What do we give him?" Miranda asked.

"Lava lamps make good gifts," Gordo suggested.

Miranda and Lizzie gave Gordo a *Look*. Gordo shrugged.

Honestly, Lizzie thought, Gordo is cool, but sometimes he's a little out there.

Finally, the three friends peeked out of the huddle. Matt was staring at them, his arms folded across his chest.

Lizzie planted her hands on her hips. "What do you want?" she snapped.

"I want to come with," Matt said.

Lizzie rolled her eyes. "No."

"Yes." Matt didn't move.

Okay, he isn't giving in, Lizzie thought. We need a new strategy. Gordo, Miranda, and Lizzie huddled up again.

"He's *not* coming with," Lizzie insisted.

"He's got to," Gordo insisted. "He's the only one who knows where it is."

"He did pass as a supergenius at school for half a day," Miranda reminded Lizzie.

Lizzie rolled her eyes. Ugh, don't remind me, she thought as her mind flashed back to that horrible day when Matt showed up at her school and passed himself off as Matt Bond, child billionaire/choreographer/movie mogul extraordinaire.

Gordo jerked his head toward Matt. "His quirky charm could be useful," he suggested.

Lizzie could see that there was no way she was going to win this battle. "Fine," she said at last.

The friends broke their huddle and turned back to face Matt.

"You can come," Lizzie told him.

Miranda folded her arms across her chest. "So tell us where it is," she said.

"The Ren-Mar Warehouses," Matt said, pointing to one of the only places on the map that *wasn't* marked with a red X.

"Thanks," Lizzie said snidely as she flounced toward her door. "Have fun hanging with Mom and Dad tomorrow."

Miranda and Gordo followed her out of the room. Gordo chuckled and mussed Matt's hair.

"If you ditch me," Matt called after them, "I'll rat you out."

Just when i thought i was out, he pulls me back in!

Lizzie's shoulders slumped. She and her friends turned back toward Matt.

Matt lifted his eyebrows. "I thought you'd see it my way," he said with a sly grin.

"Fine," Lizzie snapped. "Tomorrow morning. Early. In the backyard." She glared at Matt. "Don't wake the 'rents."

Miranda elbowed Lizzie in the side. Lizzie sighed and gave Miranda a what-can-I-do? look. After all, it wasn't like Matt was giving her a choice. Lizzie walked out of the room.

Miranda followed, but first she scrunched up her face and narrowed her eyes at Matt.

Matt shrugged and took a bite of his pizza.

Like it or not, Lizzie thought, Toad-Boy is on board.

CHAPTER TWO

"I thought you'd never get home," Mrs. McGuire said as her husband trudged into the kitchen. "You must be exhausted."

"I am exhausted," Mr. McGuire said as he plopped his briefcase on the kitchen island.

"Are you hungry?" Mrs. McGuire asked. "There's leftover pizza." She nodded at the two slices of pizza beside her. She had hidden them when the pizza arrived so that Lizzie and her friends wouldn't gobble up every last bite.

Mr. McGuire shook his head. "No, I had dinner with a client."

"Who?" Mrs. McGuire asked.

"McMorrow," Lizzie's dad said. "That guy never stops talking. But, you know, he gave me these backstage passes to Zander Knight." Mr. McGuire reached into his jacket pocket and pulled out a couple of blue laminated badges.

Mrs. McGuire looked down at the passes, which read WINTER WONDER-LAND VIDEO PASS. AUTHORIZED RESTRICTED AREAS.

Mr. McGuire frowned at the passes. "Think the kids will want them?" he asked.

"Great," Mrs. McGuire said, smiling at her husband. "We'll surprise them in the morning. They'll love 'em."

Lizzie yawned. It was seven in the morning, and she was standing in her backyard with

Gordo and Miranda, shivering in the cool spring air.

People shouldn't be allowed to get up this early on a Saturday, Lizzie thought. Still, she was wide awake. Probably from all of the nervous energy she'd stored up. She was way excited—today was the day she was going to meet Zander Knight!

In spite of the horrifyingly early hour, her best friends were ready to go. Gordo was holding his video camera, which was loaded with fresh film. Miranda had on a supercute outfit—an orange halter, blue sweater, and dark blue pleather pants—perfect for a singing audition. Her hair was even done up in little pigtails on the top of her head, some of the dark strands streaked with blue.

Lizzie was ready, too. She had taped her name on her reporter's tape recorder so that she could show Zander Knight how official she was. Lizzie just hoped she had thought of everything.

"Okay," Lizzie announced, "I left a note saying that I'm working on a project with you guys and Matt's helping. Do we have everything?"

Gordo nodded toward his video camera. "Camera and an extra battery," he said. "Check."

"Cool." Lizzie nodded and held up her tape recorder. "I've got my tape recorder for the interview and my school press badge. That should be enough to get us in."

"So what's the plan?" Gordo asked.

Lizzie shrugged. "We'll just breeze through Security like we own the place."

Gordo raised his eyebrows dubiously. "That's the plan?"

Lizzie folded her arms across her chest. "Do you have a better one?" she asked.

"No," Gordo admitted.

"Then that's the plan," Lizzie told him.

Just then, Matt walked out onto the deck, dragging a huge white laundry sack over his shoulder.

Lizzie sighed. "Oh. Great," she said in a bored voice. "You made it."

Gordo cocked an eyebrow. "What's in the bag?"

Matt pointed at Lizzie and her friends. "Do you guys have a plan?" he asked.

Miranda scowled at him. "Yeah," she said defensively.

Matt held out his laundry sack. "Then this is for when *your* plan fails."

Lizzie had to press her lips together to keep herself from growling at her little brother. Seriously—how did he ever get so annoying? I hope there isn't any trace of Matt's personality in my gene pool, Lizzie thought. I'd hate to pass it on to any of my children.

Who'd want to hang out with kids like that?

Lizzie, Gordo, Miranda, and Matt pedaled across town toward the Ren-Mar Warehouses and ditched their bikes at the back of a nearby drugstore. They could see the security gate from halfway up the block. The place was definitely hopping—it looked as though Matt had been right about the video location.

"Okay, remember," Lizzie whispered to her friends—and Matt—as they crept along the wall outside the warehouses, "walk in like you own the place."

Miranda looked at the ground. "Zander Knight walked on this ground!" she squealed. "I am never wearing these shoes again." Miranda pulled off her orange platforms.

Gordo lifted his eyebrows at her. "That's not acting like you own the place."

Miranda rolled her eyes. In her view, Gordo would just never understand these things.

At Lizzie's nod, the foursome fell into step, strolling confidently toward the security gate. Miranda swung her shoes at her sides. Only a few steps more and we'll be face-to-face with Zander Knight! Lizzie thought, giddily.

Suddenly, a burly security guard stepped in front of them. He was holding a plate that was piled high with eggs and sausages. Lizzie and her friends tripped over one another to avoid running into him.

"'Scuse me?" the guard said, frowning at them over a forkful of sausage. "May I see your passes please?"

"Let me handle this," Lizzie said as she nudged Gordo out of the way and walked confidently up to the security guard. She pulled out the press pass that Mr. Lang had just run through the school laminating machine the week before. "I'm Lizzie McGuire," Lizzie said in her most I'm-a-very-busy-and-important-person voice, "a member of the press—" She flashed her badge at the guard. "I have a right to be here."

The security guard took her press badge. He didn't look impressed.

Lizzie swallowed hard. Maybe this plan wasn't so great, after all.

Mrs. McGuire sat at the butcher-block kitchen island, sipping a cup of coffee and peering at the note that Lizzie had left that morning.

i'm working on a project with Miranda and Gordo. Matt's also helping. We'll be back soon.
Love, Lizzie

Mrs. McGuire sighed. "Well," she said to her husband, "looks like the kids got an early start this morning."

Mr. McGuire frowned. "When are they coming back?"

Mrs. McGuire took another sip of coffee. "Probably soon," Mrs. McGuire guessed. Lizzie's note was pretty vague. "Why don't you head down to the video shoot and I'll just bring them when they get back."

Mr. McGuire flipped his hair and grinned. "I can't believe I'm gonna meet Zander Knight!" he squealed.

His wife gaped at him.

"I'm just practicing so I'll fit in with the kids," Mr. McGuire explained.

Mrs. McGuire smiled and took yet another sip of coffee. She'd have to drink a lot of the stuff before *she* was that excited to meet Zander Knight.

❊ ❊ ❊

"Great plan, McGuire," Gordo said sarcastically.

The foursome slumped against a wall—outside the warehouses. The guard hadn't let them in. In fact, he had taken Lizzie's press badge away. Now they had no way to get inside, and absolutely no plan. Lizzie sighed. This wasn't going as smoothly as she had hoped.

Gordo looked over at Miranda. "Would you put your shoes on?" he snapped, eyeing her bare feet.

Miranda sighed and reached for her platforms.

"I cannot believe that they took my press badge!" Lizzie complained. "Mr. Lang charges us five bucks to replace it."

"I'm never gonna get to sing for Zander," Miranda moaned as she pulled her shoes back on.

Lizzie's little brother was the only one who didn't seem dejected. He hauled the white laundry sack he'd brought along onto his lap. "It's time for plan B," he announced. Then he rummaged around in the bag and pulled out a goofy green vest.

Gordo stared at him. "Elf costumes?" he demanded. "That's plan B?"

Lizzie poured all of her energy into not strangling Matt. Does he have to pick right now to be totally weird? she thought angrily. Can't he wait until we get home?

That's it. Matt's goin' in the bag.

Lizzie curled her lip as she snatched the ugly elf costume out of Matt's hand. "Where did you get this?" she asked.

"The Christmas Card picture we had to take last year," Matt said.

Of course, Lizzie thought. How could I have forgotten? Her dad had made the whole family get dressed up in these ridiculous costumes while he posed for the picture in a Santa suit. Lizzie had refused to even *look* at the photos on the basis that it was bad for her mental health, so her mom had forged Lizzie's signature on all of the cards. What a very merry year *that* had been.

"I am not singing for Zander dressed as an elf," Miranda insisted, scowling at the outfit.

"Guys, they're shooting a holiday video," Matt explained. "If you look like elves, they'll think we're part of the video."

Wow. Monkey-Boy makes sense.

Lizzie cocked an eyebrow at Matt as he handed out the elf outfits. "Who are you going as?" Lizzie asked, reluctantly taking the costume. "Santa Claus?"

Matt grinned. "Nope." He reached into the bag and pulled out a pair of black pants, a black shirt, and a blond wig.

"Those are *my* pants!" Lizzie cried, eyeing the pleather.

Matt grinned. "I'm going as Zander Knight," he said as he pulled on the wig.

Lizzie rolled her eyes. This plan is so goofy, it has to work, she thought. Besides—it was the only plan they had.

CHAPTER THREE

Lizzie, Gordo, and Miranda pulled the elf costumes on over their clothes while Matt changed into his Zander Knight outfit. Lizzie helped him straighten his wig. Then all four of them walked up to Security as nonchalantly as possible.

The guard has to believe we're in the video, Lizzie thought. After all, our elf outfits *do* look pretty official—red shirts, red pants, green vest, red pointy-toed shoes, and even red caps with red pom-poms on top.

This time, the burly security guard was eating a banana as he stopped them. "'Scuse me?" he said as Lizzie and company tried to walk past him. "Do you have your passes?"

Lizzie stopped in her tracks. Stay cool, she told herself. Just act like you belong. She folded her arms across her chest. "We're extras in the Zander Knight video," Lizzie said smoothly.

"Yeah!" Miranda chimed in.

"And we're late," Gordo said in his fake official voice. "So can we shake a leg, buddy?"

The guard eyed their elf outfits skeptically and gestured toward the street. "Scram," he said as he shooed them away. "Nice try."

Matt was the only one who refused to budge. "Do you know who I am?" he demanded.

The guard gestured toward the street with his banana. "See ya," he said.

Just then, a production assistant wearing a headset trotted up to Matt and grabbed him by the shoulders. "I got him," the P.A. said into his headset. "I've got him." He turned to Matt and frowned. "Stand-ins must stay on set at all times," he said firmly as he steered Matt away, past the guard and onto Zander Knight's set! "Let's go."

Matt just shrugged and let himself be led along.

Lizzie couldn't believe this! Her brother's plan had actually worked! But only for *him*!

"Plan B didn't work," Miranda said morosely as she, Lizzie, and Gordo sat slumped against the side of one of the Ren-Mar Warehouses.

"It worked for Matt," Lizzie said, trying to keep the bitterness out of her voice. Not to mention the fact that he gets to wear my pleather pants while I'm stuck in this stupid elf costume, she added mentally, eyeing her curly-toed shoes.

"Maybe in our next plan we could pretend that we're elves who live in trees and bake cookies," Gordo said.

Lizzie glared at him. "Not helpful, Gordo."

"Maybe we should just pack it in," Miranda said sadly.

"No." Lizzie's voice was firm. She had come this far—and she wasn't about to give up. Especially not when Matt was already inside, hanging with Zander Knight! "We are getting in," Lizzie declared. "Okay. I'm going to get my interview." She pointed at Miranda. "You're going to sing for Zander, and Gordo's going to film it."

We're goin' in, and this time we're not leaving anyone behind!

At that moment, a silver station wagon drove up, honking. It looked a lot like her parents' car, but she didn't think much about that. At the time, all she cared about was its strategic position right next to the security station outside the warehouses.

"I've got an idea," Lizzie said quickly. "Follow me."

Lizzie, Gordo, and Miranda ducked down and crept alongside the stopped car. The vehicle totally blocked the security guard's view of them!

I just hope no one spots these brilliant red and green elf outfits, Lizzie thought as she huddled below the car's passenger-side window. Suddenly, Lizzie had a thought. Omigosh, she mused, what if Zander Knight is *in* this very car? The idea was so thrilling that Lizzie just couldn't contain herself. She peeked into the car. But the man behind the wheel was definitely *not* Zander Knight—or anyone Zander Knight would ever hang out with. To tell the truth, he looked like a bit of a nerd. That guy looks just like my dad, Lizzie thought.

"Gotta pass?" asked the burly guard, who was holding an ice-cream cone.

"Yeah," the guy in the car said. He reached for his pass and looked right at Lizzie.

Lizzie ducked.

Omigosh! Lizzie realized. That *is* my dad!

Mr. McGuire frowned at the vision of his daughter that had just disappeared from his car window. He shook his head, then dug around for his all-access pass and held it out to the guard. Lizzie's dad looked back at the window. Lizzie was definitely not there. "Nah," he said to himself.

The security guard stared at the pass for a long time. Finally, he nodded—satisfied. "All right," he said, waving Mr. McGuire along, "move through."

Mr. McGuire drove into the warehouse complex.

Using the car as camouflage, Lizzie and her friends sneaked by the guard. Once they were well inside the complex, they pressed themselves against a wall, hoping to keep out of sight. Not an easy task when you're wearing a goofy elf outfit.

"Lizzie!" Miranda whispered fiercely. "That was your dad!"

"Security must've called him!" Gordo said reasonably. "They do have your press badge!"

"Okay, new plan," Lizzie said in a low

voice. "Find Zander, get Matt, avoid Dad, and get out."

No problemo. I can do four things at once.

"Whew—we made it!" Miranda said as she, Lizzie, and Gordo trotted down a flight of stairs into the main warehouse area. Miranda looked around eagerly. "Where's Zander?"

"First things first." Gordo gestured toward his hideous elf clothes. The friends pulled off the ugly outfits as quickly as they could. "Let's ditch these costumes."

"Good idea," Lizzie agreed. She and Gordo handed their elf costumes to Miranda, who stuffed them into a nearby garbage can. Good riddance, Lizzie thought as she tossed in her hat with the red pom-pom. There was no way she was meeting Zander Knight in *that* outfit.

"Gordo," Miranda said as her eyes flicked to his video camera, "did you get a shot of us sneaking in for your documentary?"

Gordo shook his head. "No, I was too busy trying not to get arrested."

"Well," Lizzie said as she peered around, "the coast is clear. Get a shot of us right now." Lizzie pulled Miranda to the side. Gordo held up his video camera, and the girls smiled into the lens.

Gordo focused in on Lizzie and Miranda . . . and noticed someone else in the background. Suddenly, Gordo pulled the camera away from his face. "Uh, guys?" he said. "This is about to be the shortest documentary ever."

"Not you again!" shouted a voice.

Lizzie turned and saw the beefy security guard. She and Miranda screamed as the guard lunged at them. Lizzie didn't have time to think—she just started running. Miranda and Gordo were right behind her.

The guard took off after them, not even stopping to put down the plate of food in his hand.

Lizzie dodged through the warehouse complex as quickly as she could. Luckily, the security guard was pretty slow. *I guess all of those carbs finally caught up with him!* thought Lizzie as she ran up the stairs. The guard had to stop to catch his breath.

Lizzie and her friends trotted into another warehouse, and walked right up to a long table covered with fruit, cheese, doughnuts, and other goodies. A group of girl elves in cool-looking, sleek outfits were walking around.

Those must be the dancers for the video, Lizzie realized. *No wonder our elf outfits didn't fit in—all of these elves look totally hot!* Across the room, Lizzie could see a big

Santa sleigh full of wrapped gifts. Lizzie stopped in her tracks. This was it! She was actually on the set of Zander Knight's holiday video.

"Yum," Lizzie said, eyeing the goodies on the table. "I cannot believe that Matt was right."

Gordo's eyes went wide at the sight of the food. "Mmmm . . . doughnuts."

"We did it!" Miranda cried happily. "We made it. We're here."

Lizzie nodded and grabbed Miranda's hand. "Cool—let's find Zander." She headed toward the stage door, but stopped. A familiar face had just walked in.

Lizzie and her friends ducked behind the giant Santa sleigh as the guard walked over to the food table. So that's where he's been getting all of those snacks, Lizzie realized.

"Basically, it's a television series about a dad

and his wacky life," Mr. McGuire said to a tall man in a chef's white jacket and hat. They were both walking toward the food table. "I call it *Sam McGuire*." Lizzie's dad waggled his eyebrows. "Whaddya think?"

The man in the chef's hat sighed. "Sir," he said, "I'm the caterer." Then he put a plate of brownies on the table.

Lizzie and her friends looked at one another. They had to get away from Lizzie's dad and that security guard or they would be stone-cold busted! Desperate, Lizzie looked around the video set. There had to be some place to hide. . . . Of course! she realized as she looked at the Santa sleigh—*the answer is right in front of me.*

"Okay, get in the bag!" Lizzie whispered, pointing to the toy sack in the back of the sleigh. "In the bag! Now!"

The friends didn't waste any time—they

scrambled into the sack. It was big enough for all three of them—barely.

Lizzie peeked out of the top of the bag. What was her dad doing now?

Mr. McGuire looked at the brownies that the caterer had just placed on the table, then noticed the rest of the snacks. "Mmmmm . . . doughnuts," he said, reaching for one.

The caterer snatched the doughnut out of his hand with a pair of tongs. "Those are for crew only," the caterer said, using the doughnut to gesture toward a sign that read CREW ONLY.

Lizzie felt something move beneath her. Oh, no! Some members of the crew were pushing the Santa sleigh somewhere. Where are they taking us? Lizzie wondered. She didn't really care, as long as it wasn't to Security. Lizzie had definitely seen enough of that beefy guard for one day.

CHAPTER FOUR

Mrs. McGuire walked into the kitchen, biting her lip. She just couldn't figure out where Lizzie and Matt could be. She had already called Miranda's and Gordo's houses. Then Mrs. McGuire had dashed over to the library and to the Digital Bean, Lizzie's favorite cybercafé. But Lizzie and her friends—and Matt—were nowhere to be found.

"They're not at Gordo's," Mrs. McGuire said to herself. "They're not at Miranda's—

they know they're supposed to leave a number." She was starting to worry. Just then, Mrs. McGuire noticed the light on the answering machine was blinking. She punched the PLAY button impatiently.

"Hello." The answering machine made the security guard's voice sound tinny. "This is Security from Ren-Mar Warehouses. We got a Lizzie McGuire here causing some trouble."

Mrs. McGuire closed her eyes. Then she took a deep breath and stormed out the door.

That security guard didn't know the meaning of the word trouble.

"The sleigh stopped," Miranda said.

Lizzie tried to shift her position. It wasn't easy—the three friends were squished together like cotton balls at the top of a bottle of aspirin. Not to mention the fact that there was a pile of wrapped boxes crowded onto their laps.

"I can't feel my foot," Gordo complained.

"You guys," Lizzie whispered, "I think we're onstage."

"Yeah," Gordo went on. "My foot's definitely asleep."

"Let me just take a peek." Lizzie peered through the opening at the top of the sack. A blond guy in an all-black outfit was standing with the director. His back was to her . . . but it was a back that definitely seemed familiar. "Guys," Lizzie said breathlessly as she ducked back into the bag, "Zander Knight's here!"

"Of course, he is," Gordo said. "It's his video."

Miranda ignored him. "What do we do?" she asked Lizzie.

"Um . . . I have a plan," Lizzie said. "Follow me."

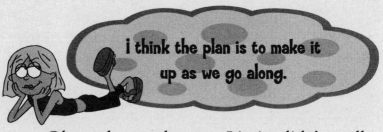

i think the plan is to make it up as we go along.

Okay, the truth was, Lizzie didn't really have a plan. But she did know one thing—nothing cool was going to happen to her and her friends if they just sat around, smooshed together inside a giant sack of toys.

Lizzie poked her head out of the sack, and she and her friends instantly found themselves in the middle of a winter wonderland. There were fake snowdrifts, giant candy canes, enormous lollipops, and huge snowflakes everywhere. A few elf dancers started walking onto the stage.

"ACTION!" the director shouted. "Cue the dancers!"

Miranda's dark eyebrows flew up. "Dancers?" she repeated.

"Oh, this can't be good," Gordo said.

Lizzie and her friends tried to run toward the side of the stage, but a group of elf dancers was in their way. In fact, elf dancers had suddenly appeared everywhere. Lizzie, Miranda, and Gordo were trapped!

"Sorry," Lizzie said as she bumped into a cute elf. "Sorry."

Suddenly, all of the elf dancers crouched in a line at the front of the stage. Lizzie, Miranda, and Gordo were the only ones left standing. Lizzie had never thought she would want her hideous elf outfit back, but right now, she would have given anything to have that stupid hat with the tassel on it. At least then maybe I'd fit in, Lizzie thought—kind of.

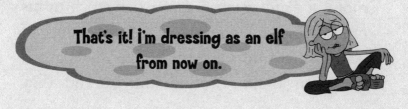

That's it! i'm dressing as an elf from now on.

"CUT!" the director shouted. "Where are your costumes?" He strode over to Lizzie and her friends.

Oh no, Lizzie thought. I can't believe I'm meeting Zander this way. Still, Lizzie couldn't help taking a peek at the star. . . .

"Matt?" Lizzie asked, gaping at the blond boy. Or rather, the boy in the blond wig.

"Lizzie?" Matt said.

Just then, the security guard walked onto the set behind them. "We meet again!" the guard said, lunging toward Lizzie, Gordo, and Miranda.

"Aaaaaaaaahhh!" Lizzie shouted, and she and her friends bolted off the stage.

The security guard chased them across the room, a giant chicken drumstick stuck in his mouth. Lizzie, Miranda, and Gordo ducked behind a white Christmas tree. The guard darted at them. Around and around they went. The guard lunged at them again, and the kids ducked the other way. Suddenly, Lizzie had an idea. She looked at her friends and nodded.

"Timber!" Gordo called as he shoved the tree over . . . right onto the guard!

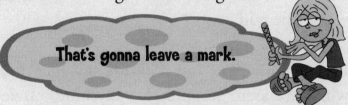

That's gonna leave a mark.

"We're really sorry!" Lizzie called over her shoulder as she, Miranda, and Gordo scurried away.

"I'm gonna get you kids!" the guard screeched as he lay on his back, flailing. His drumstick was covered in fake snow.

The video director stared at the scene with wide eyes. "Did you know those kids?" the director asked Matt.

"Never seen 'em in my life," Matt told him.

The director shook his head slightly. "Too bad. I can always use more stunt elves."

"You know," Matt said quickly, "now that I think about it, I taught them everything they know."

The director nodded at Matt. "Good work," he said.

Lizzie, Miranda, and Gordo ran like the wind. We aren't stopping for anything, Lizzie thought as she and her friends darted past a couple of music executives.

Gordo stopped in his tracks. "Excuse me," he said smoothly, "but if you guys ever need a fresh new video director . . ." He handed one of the executives a card.

Lizzie rolled her eyes. She and Miranda hustled Gordo away. He was still shouting, "I've got a unique and youthful point of view!"

Okay, we have to hide, Lizzie thought as

she, Gordo, and Miranda ducked behind a couple of huge snowflakes. This is good, Lizzie thought, just as two burly stagehands walked up and carried the snowflakes away, revealing them. Okay, this is bad, Lizzie thought. Time for the next plan.

Lizzie led her friends to an elaborate doorway with the words "Santa's House" arching over it. Maybe we can hide in here, Lizzie thought as she yanked open the door. But there was nothing on the other side. "Santa's House" wasn't a house at all—it was just a door. And it led them right back to the music executives.

Lizzie sighed. That's the biggest problem with this music video, she thought. There aren't enough good hiding places!

Mrs. McGuire pulled up to the security station. "Hi, I'm Jo McGuire," she said to the guard in the calmest voice she could muster.

"I spoke to you earlier about my daughter, Lizzie McGuire."

"Yes, ma'am," the guard said. He twirled a piece of strawberry licorice in Mrs. McGuire's face. "She's caused quite a ruckus today." He was still aching where the fake Christmas tree had fallen on him.

"I'm really sorry," Mrs. McGuire said. She was trying to be polite—she really was. She just wanted to find her children *right away*. "Could you take me to Lizzie?"

"The problem is," the guard admitted, "we don't know where Lizzie is." He poked Mrs. McGuire's arm with the licorice.

"Okay," Mrs. McGuire said. Her voice was quavering with impatience. "Why don't you let me in and I'll find her," she suggested.

The guard shook his head. "Can't let you in, ma'am." He poked her again. *Poke, poke.*

That was when Mrs. McGuire lost it.

"You're gonna let me in!" she screamed, grabbing the guard by the collar. "And you're gonna let me in now! You understand?!"

Finally, Lizzie spotted an office. That could be a good place to hide, Lizzie thought. She jerked her head toward it, and Gordo nodded. Lizzie yanked open the door, and her friends followed her inside. There was a comfy-looking couch and a coffee table with a basket of fruit on it.

"We are never going to meet Zander Knight." Miranda groaned as she flopped on the couch.

"Maybe we should just call it a day," Gordo suggested as he sat down next to Miranda.

"But we're so close," Lizzie insisted. She flopped onto the couch, too. This crazy day had given her a headache. "Just give me a minute to think."

i got nothin'.

Exhausted, Lizzie leaned back. "Arrgh!" she cried, tucking a strand of hair behind her ear. She had to come up with a plan. She just had to. Maybe if we can get back onto the set, Lizzie thought, we can hide in the sleigh again until Zander shows up. "All we need to do is get—" Lizzie started, but suddenly, her eye fell on a blue pass hanging from the lamp next to her. ZANDER KNIGHT, the pass read just below a picture of the superhot star. "Zander Knight's personal pass!" Lizzie gasped.

"How are we gonna get Zander Knight's personal pass?" Gordo asked sarcastically.

Miranda grabbed the pass right out of Lizzie's hands, and stared at it as though it were made of solid gold. Then she waved it in Gordo's face. "ZANDER KNIGHT'S PERSONAL PASS!" Miranda screeched.

"I guess this must be Zander Knight's dressing room," Gordo said as he looked around the room. "Again, this would be a lot more exciting if I were a teenage girl."

Lizzie put down her tape recorder and reached for the fruit basket on the table in front of them. "And this is Zander's orange!" she cried.

"And this is Zander's apple!" Miranda added. "Ha, ha, ha, ha!"

"And this is Zander's manager wondering what you're doing here," a voice said.

Lizzie, Miranda, and Gordo looked up into the face of an ultrahip young woman. She did *not* look happy to see them.

The friends jumped off the couch and stared at one another. Lizzie gulped. What was she going to do now?

❋ ❋ ❋

Mr. McGuire had been standing by the goodies table for almost thirty minutes, and he still hadn't taken a doughnut. Even though they looked so amazingly delicious.

Mr. McGuire looked around to see if anyone was looking his way. Nope. He reached out and grabbed a fat chocolate one.

"Sir, are you part of the crew?" the security guard asked, instantly appearing behind him.

Mr. McGuire sighed and moved to place the doughnut back on the table. But a moment later, he darted off, the doughnut still clenched tightly in his hand.

He didn't get far.

The security guard hauled Mr. McGuire into the holding room, where Mrs. McGuire was sitting on the floor, bouncing a rubber ball off the wall.

"Oh my gosh!" she said when she saw her

husband. "It's about time you got here!" Mrs. McGuire scrambled to her feet.

The security guard slammed the door shut.

"Listen, Lizzie and Matt are here," Mrs. McGuire went on. "We've gotta go find them!"

Mr. McGuire sat down on the bench that was built into the wall. His wife sat down beside him. Suddenly, her hopeful face fell. "You're not here to bail me out, are you?"

Mr. McGuire wrinkled his nose. "They're real persnickety about their doughnuts around here."

"Doughnuts!" Mrs. McGuire yelled. "We've got to find the kids."

Mr. McGuire shrugged. He wasn't worried. "If Security's that good at policing the dough-nut table, it's only a matter of time before the kids join us."

CHAPTER FIVE

"I won't call the security guard if you guys leave immediately," Zander Knight's manager said.

"Just wait a second," Lizzie pleaded. "Okay? In the spirit of Christmas, maybe you could grant us one favor?"

"Tell me what you want," the manager said.

Lizzie smiled. She couldn't believe that "spirit of Christmas" line had worked on the woman! "We want to meet Zander Knight," Lizzie said quickly.

"Um . . ." The manager looked at the ceiling, thinking.

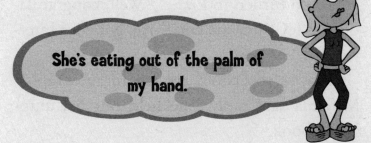

She's eating out of the palm of my hand.

"No," the manager said with a raise of her eyebrows. This was obviously her final answer.

Ow!

Lizzie's face fell. "Okay, just hear me out," she begged. "Zander Knight's coming here is the most exciting thing that's ever happened to us. He's cute, he's cool, he's talented, so, please, please . . . can *one* of us just meet him?"

The manager sighed. "Okay," she said finally. "Just one."

Gordo turned to Lizzie. "Well, congratulations, McGuire," he said. "You got your interview."

"Maybe you could get me an autograph?" Miranda said sadly. She held out her autograph book.

Lizzie's heart lurched. She really, really wanted to meet Zander Knight. But she knew, at that moment, she wasn't going to. "Miranda, you should go," Lizzie said softly.

Miranda's jaw dropped. "What?"

"You're a really good singer," Lizzie said, "and this is a great opportunity for you. So go." She glanced toward the manager.

"Are you sure?" Miranda asked.

Please, just go before I totally change my mind! Lizzie thought. But she knew she wouldn't change her mind—not really.

This was too important for Miranda.

"Yeah," Lizzie said. "I'm sure." She smiled. "Maybe you could get me an autograph."

Find out what he sleeps in!

Miranda laughed, and Lizzie reached out for a hug. Gordo smiled. It was the first time she'd seen him smile all day, Lizzie thought as she and Miranda embraced.

Lizzie, Gordo, and Miranda followed Zander's manager out the dressing room's back door. After ten minutes, the manager came out again and ushered Miranda inside to meet him.

"Lizzie," Gordo said, once they were outside, "I gotta say, what you did in there was really cool."

Lizzie shrugged. "Well, this is a once-in-a-lifetime chance for Miranda."

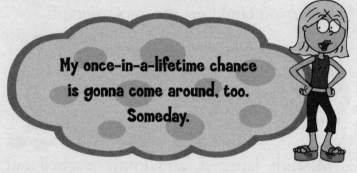

My once-in-a-lifetime chance is gonna come around, too. Someday.

Just then, Miranda walked out of Zander's dressing room. She took a deep breath, then grinned dreamily.

"How was it?" Lizzie asked quickly. "Tell me *everything*!"

"He said I have talent," Miranda gushed. "*I* have talent!" Miranda swallowed hard and smiled at her best friend. "Lizzie, there's no way I'll ever be able to thank you. You're the best."

Lizzie grinned. She was sad that she didn't

get to meet Zander Knight, but seeing Miranda looking so happy was definitely worth it.

"I wonder if those two record executives are still around?" Gordo said.

Miranda rolled her eyes.

"Oh my gosh," Lizzie said suddenly. "You guys, where's my tape recorder?" She looked around—none of them had it. "I think I left it in Zander's dressing room!" Lizzie scratched her head. "Should I go back?"

"I'm sure it's okay," Gordo said. "We'll wait here."

Lizzie walked back to Zander Knight's dressing room. She hesitated a moment, then knocked softly.

Zander Knight opened the door.

Lizzie had to catch her breath. Zander Knight. He is right here in front of me, Lizzie thought. And he's holding my tape recorder!

She could see her name written across the front in bold letters.

"Is this yours?" Zander asked, glancing at the tape recorder.

Lizzie nodded, momentarily speechless. "Thanks," she managed to say as he handed it to her.

"Merry Christmas, Lizzie McGuire," Zander said.

He knows my name! Lizzie thought. That was when she noticed that Zander was staring at something over her head. Lizzie looked up. There was a sprig of mistletoe hung over Zander's doorway.

What's that doing there? Lizzie thought dimly . . . just as Zander Knight leaned over and kissed her.

Zander smiled. Then he closed the door.

Lizzie felt faint. Her brain could barely manage to command her legs to move forward—but somehow, she managed to walk back toward her friends.

"So, did you get your tape recorder?" Gordo asked.

"That's not all I got," Lizzie replied, grinning.

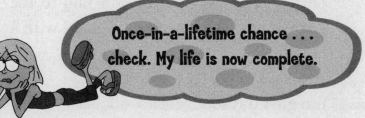

Once-in-a-lifetime chance . . . check. My life is now complete.

Suddenly, a speaker crackled. "Will Lizzie McGuire please pick up your parents at the detention center?" a voice boomed over the loudspeaker.

"I guess my parents aren't going anywhere for a while," Lizzie said with a smile.

"And neither are you," said the security guard as he walked up to them. "Come with me," he commanded. "Now."

"Hang on a sec." Lizzie looked over and saw the video director walking toward her. Matt was with him. "These your friends?" the director asked Matt.

"Yup," Matt said smoothly. "The greatest stunt elves in the business."

"They're with us," the director said to the security guard. He dismissed the guard with a little hand wave.

The guard's eyes grew round.

"You guys did some great work back there," the director said to Lizzie and her friends.

It took Lizzie a minute to realize that he was talking about their crazy Christmas-tree chase.

"How would you like to be in Zander Knight's video?" the director asked.

Lizzie, Miranda, and Gordo stared at one another, speechless. The guard was speechless, too.

The director smiled. "I'll take that as a yes."

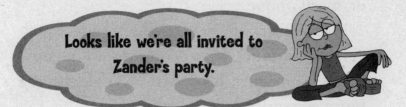

Looks like we're all invited to Zander's party.

A few minutes later, Lizzie found herself back on the set for Zander Knight's video. There was the same fake snow, Santa sleigh, and dancing elves . . . but this time, Lizzie and Miranda *belonged* there. The stylist had given them cute holiday outfits—Miranda wore a silver velvet shirt and a red skirt, and Lizzie had on a red sweater and cool gold pants— and the choreographer had shown them a couple of dance moves.

"Places!" the director shouted, and everyone rushed to their marks. "Action!" he cried, and suddenly, the dancing elves parted to reveal Zander Knight himself, dressed in a hip silver parka and silver pants. He was chatting on a cell phone.

"Hey, Billy?" he said as the music blared. "Hey, it's Zander. I can't come over. I'm going to see someone. It's a girl." Suddenly, the music intensified. Zander put down his cell phone and grabbed a microphone. "I'm going to see a girl. A very special girl," Zander sang as he and the dancing elves moved to the music of his huge hit, "Special Girl."

Lizzie and Miranda moved to the beat, just the way the choreographer had showed them, as Zander went through the song. He even came over and sang just to them!

Matt sneaked onstage and went into his famous robot-dance. Lizzie ignored him, but the director loved it. Oh, well, Lizzie decided. I don't care if Matt's in the video, too. Let's face it—if it weren't for Toad-Boy, I wouldn't be here!

Lizzie just kept dancing. Everyone was

loving the song—even the security guard got into the beat.

Lizzie was smiling like crazy as she and Miranda lip-synched the chorus to the song. I've never had so much fun in my life! Lizzie thought.

Gordo stood in front of them, next to the cameras. He was finally filming his own "making of" video. Lizzie hoped that he was getting some good footage . . . and that he was having as much fun as she and Miranda were.

Lizzie couldn't believe that everything had worked out perfectly. She had met Zander Knight, got to be in his video—*and* didn't even have to dress as an elf!

Hey, Lizzie thought as she danced away next to the giant candy canes, who says Christmas wishes can't come true?

Don't close the book on Lizzie yet!
Here's a sneak peek at the next
Lizzie McGuire story. . . .

Adapted by Jasmine Jones
Based on the series created by Terri Minsky
Based on a teleplay written
by Douglas Tuber & Tim Maile

"**M**ail's here," Mrs. McGuire said as she strode out onto the patio.

Lizzie McGuire looked up eagerly at her mom. But Mrs. McGuire sorted through the stack of envelopes without even glancing in Lizzie's direction.

Sighing, Lizzie leaned against her lounge chair and went back to leafing through the fashion magazine in her lap. Why do I even bother getting my hopes up? Lizzie wondered. I never get any mail. Sometimes I wonder whether people even know that I live here. It's like I don't exist!

"Here you go," Mrs. McGuire said as she passed Lizzie's dad a small bundle of mail. He and Lizzie's annoying little brother, Matt, had been fixing Matt's old bike. Both of them were covered in grease. Mr. McGuire left black fingerprints on the envelopes as he flipped through them.

"Oh, good. Property tax bill," Mr. McGuire said sarcastically. He flipped to the next envelope in the pile.

Lizzie smiled a little behind her magazine.

Okay, so there were some things that were worse than getting *no* mail.

"Matt got something from Gammy McGuire." Mrs. McGuire passed Matt a thick yellow envelope; then she looked down at what was left in her hands. "That's all junk," she said, flipping through it. "Junk, junk, junk."

Matt ripped open his card. "Cool!" he squealed. "A fifty-dollar gift certificate for my birthday!"

"But your birthday was seven months ago," Mr. McGuire said, clearly confused. He turned to his wife. "Gammy got him a baseball glove, right?" he asked.

Mrs. McGuire peered at him over the top of her square glasses. "Your mother sends him birthday presents every six weeks now," she said, then turned back to her enormous stack of junk mail. "She's getting a little . . . fuzzy around the edges."

Lizzie listened to this conversation distract-edly as she peered at her magazine. Personally, she *liked* getting a birthday present from her grandmother every six weeks. It made a girl feel special.

Suddenly, Lizzie's eye fell on a full-page ad of a bunch of girls in cute dresses. They were running down the beach together. "Do you have Teen Attitude?" the ad read. "Then try out for our latest fashion show!" The address for the tryout was a store at the local mall. And it wasn't just any store—the fashion show was going to be held at Cielo Drive, home of the most bangin' outfits in town. Lizzie could hardly ever afford to buy any-thing there, but she liked to visit the shop on Saturdays and drool over the clothes.

"Hey, Mom, can I be a model?" Lizzie asked.

"Sure," Matt said, "and I can be president of the moon."

"Fine," Lizzie quipped, "as long as you move there."

Leaning forward, Lizzie showed her mom the ad and said, "*Teen Attitude* magazine is putting on a fashion show at Cielo Drive. If I get picked, I get five hundred dollars' worth of free merchandise."

How cool would it be to get five hundred dollars' worth of stylin' clothes? Lizzie thought. She imagined herself waltzing into school, wearing a to-die-for outfit, grinning as her snob-alicious ex-friend Kate Sanders gritted her teeth with envy. Ha!

"If I say yes, will you stop picking on your brother and do all of your homework?" Mrs. McGuire asked. She looked at her daughter expectantly.

Pffft! Like *that's* gonna happen!

"Sure," Lizzie said, smiling innocently. She sighed and leaned back in her lounge chair. "This is so cool," she said happily. "I'm going to be a model!"

Matt lifted his eyebrows at her. "I got fifty bucks," he said.

Lizzie rolled her eyes. Okay, so she wished she'd gotten fifty bucks in the mail, too. But modeling would be way cooler.

If it worked out.

"So they just had me walk down the catwalk and spin around twice," Lizzie explained to her two best friends, Miranda Sanchez and David "Gordo" Gordon, as they headed down the hallway at school the next day.

"Let me get this straight," Gordo said, frowning slightly. "You're going to be in a fashion show?"

"Yup," Lizzie told him. "And I get five hundred dollars' worth of free merchandise."

Miranda lifted her dark eyebrows, clearly impressed.

"Five hundred simoleons," Gordo repeated. "Why didn't you tell me about this thing?" he asked Lizzie accusingly.

Lizzie gave Gordo's outfit the once-over. It consisted of a wrinkled "vintage" print button-down worn over an ancient red long-sleeved shirt, which hung, untucked and sloppy-looking, over a pair of painter's pants. Gordo was not exactly a fashionista, to put it mildly. In fact, school rumors suggested the fashion police had a warrant out for his arrest.

"I didn't think you'd be very interested in a fashion show," Lizzie said, giving Gordo a dubious look.

"I wouldn't be," Gordo agreed. "But for five hundred skins, I'd volunteer for scientific experiments."

Lizzie grinned, picturing Gordo and a Labrador hooked up to some crazy brain-switching device. Then she tried to imagine Gordo strutting down the runway in a tux. Somehow, it *did* seem more likely that Gordo could make money as a guinea pig for science than as a male model.

"I thought to be a model, you had to scowl and stomp around like you own the place," Miranda said.

"I just walked," Lizzie said with a shrug. "They said I seemed like a nice, typical thirteen-year-old girl."

"You *are* a nice, typical thirteen-year-old girl," Gordo told her.

Lizzie glared at him. *Typical?* Ouch!

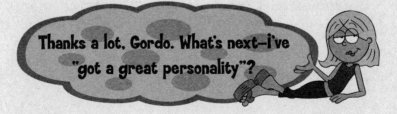

Thanks a lot, Gordo. What's next—I've "got a great personality"?

"Well, for once, being typical is finally pay-ing off," Lizzie said.

"That's good. Milk it," said a loud voice behind them. Lizzie jumped back, startled.

"Whoa! Mr. Dig," Lizzie said, recovering. Mr. Dig was a substitute teacher who always seemed to have a gig at their school. He was a hip, young African American guy, and he usu-ally came up with some pretty crazy projects for his classes. Today he was wearing a tie, which probably meant that he wasn't subbing in gym, although you never knew with Mr. Dig. "Where'd you come from?" Lizzie asked him.

"Well, my family's originally from Tobago, but I was born in East Lansing, Michigan." Mr. Dig grinned. "Go, Wolverines!"

Ohhh-kay, Lizzie thought. Whatever that means.

"So, you heard Lizzie is going to be a model?" Miranda asked.

"I did," Mr. Dig replied, nodding. "And I give her the same advice I gave supermodel Colette Romana."

Lizzie and her friends looked at one another. Who in the universe was Colette Romana?

"I told her, 'You have a natural gift. Share it with the world, and the world will love you,'" Mr. Dig said. He turned to Miranda. "Colette Romana. True story," he added, nodding with satisfaction.

Miranda uneasily adjusted the strap of her book bag. "Um . . . I've never heard of Colette Romana," she admitted.

"Well, that's because on her first photo shoot, in Nairobi, a zebra sat on her head and broke her face," Mr. Dig explained. He shook his head sadly. "Could've been famous. Tragic." He sighed and shivered at the thought.

Gordo spoke up. "Mr. Dig, I don't think you need to be famous to be happy."

"Oh, boy, please!" Mr. Dig scoffed. "You don't have to be *tall* to play in the NBA! You don't have to be *funny*-looking to be the Queen of England! You don't have to be seven hundred *pounds* to be a sumo wrestler!" He lifted his eyebrows. "But it helps."

Mr. Dig turned to Lizzie and pointed at her, a grim expression on his face. "Stay away from zebras," he advised seriously. Then he smiled. "Peace!" he chirped before flashing the peace sign and making his way down the hall.

"Shouldn't teachers be telling us that fame and money aren't important, and that we should focus on being good people?" Gordo asked, once Mr. Dig was out of earshot.

Lizzie pressed her lips together thoughtfully. Gordo was always going in for that high-ideals kind of stuff. "He's just a substitute," Lizzie pointed out after a moment. "I guess he's allowed to tell us the truth."

They all shrugged and looked at one another blankly.

Teachers, Lizzie thought. Who can figure them out?

Sorry! That's the end of the sneak peek for now. But don't go nuclear! To read the rest, all you have to do is look for the next title in the Lizzie McGuire series—

GET INSIDE HER HEAD

Lizzie McGUiRE

Weekends

Watch it on